Talent Show

Shey Kettle

illustrated by
Meredith Thomas

First published in 2006 by
MACMILLAN EDUCATION AUSTRALIA PTY LTD
627 Chapel Street, South Yarra, Australia 3141

This edition first published in the United States of America
in 2006 by MONDO Publishing.

For information contact:
MONDO Publishing
980 Avenue of the Americas
New York, NY 10018

Visit our web site at http://www.mondopub.com

06 07 08 09 10   9 8 7 6 5 4 3 2 1

ISBN 1-59336-933-6(PB)

Series created by Felice Arena and Phil Kettle
Project Management by Limelight Press Pty Ltd
Cover and text design by Lore Foye
Illustrations by Meredith Thomas

Printed in Hong Kong

GIRLZ ROCK!
CONTENTS

Mai   Carly

CHAPTER 1

The Newsletter

Carly and Mai are sitting in Mai's living room after school.

Mai "Did you see the school newsletter? The fair's coming up soon."

Carly "And we know what that means—the Annual School Talent Show!"

Mai "Yeah, where you get to perform in front of everyone and make a total idiot of yourself."

Carly "First prize is free dance lessons for a year. That'd be cool."

Mai "Yeah, totally. Let's enter—ya never know, we just might win."

Carly "Maybe I could do some hip-hop poetry or something."

Mai "Or sing. And I could do gymnastics, like flips and cartwheels."

Carly "I'd win if it were basketball or surfing."

Mai "Yeah, or fast-food eating!"

The girls keep thinking.

Carly "If we put our great talent
and great minds together, we should
be able to come up with something
that'd really rock. Then we'd win
for sure."

Mai "But seriously, what could
we do?"

Carly "I've got an idea. Do you still have your nun's outfit from that costume party we went to last year?"

Mai "Yeah, but do you want to do something as nuns? That sounds kinda lame."

Carly "No, it would be cool. Like in "The Sound of Music." Maria is a nun before she becomes a governess. And the songs in that movie are awesome. We could use some of the music from it and make up a dance routine."

Mai "Hey, yeah! Good thinking. We'll need to work out a really cool routine, but it could be totally awesome."

CHAPTER 2

Let's Do It!

The girls create their dance, using ribbons and tambourines. After hours of practice, they are ready.

Carly "I think we've got it."

Mai "Let's try the part with the star jumps one more time."

Carly "Okay. After three—one, two…"

The girls repeat the star jump sequence.

Mai "We're so good! If we win, I hope we get to choose the dance lessons we want."

Carly "What type of dancing would you want to learn? I'd like to do ballet so I could pick the other dancers up and spin them around."

Mai "You only get to do that if you're the boy. And you need to be really strong."

Carly "Well, I don't want any boy picking me up and spinning me above his head. Maybe I'll pass on the ballet."

Mai "I'd rather be a tap dancer. You can make a lot of noise when you tap dance. Let's do that."

Carly "Okay, sounds cool."

Mai climbs on the coffee table and pretends to tap dance. Carly climbs up and joins in, just as their brothers walk in the room. The boys watch for a minute, then burst out laughing.

Mai "Get lost, you two. I bet you couldn't do any better."

Mai picks up a cushion and throws
it at the boys as they disappear out
of the room.

Carly "Huh! Those boys will be in for
a surprise when they see us dance
on Saturday...and win."

Mai "We're so good we might even get our own television show."

Carly "How cool would that be—The Carly and Mai Show!"

Mai "Our act will rock. I hope we win first prize."

CHAPTER 3

Practice Makes Perfect

The day of the talent show arrives.
The girls are walking to school
together.

Mai "I feel like my stomach is full of
butterflies."

Carly "I was so nervous I could barely eat my breakfast."

Mai "Wow! You *must* be nervous. You can usually eat all day."

Carly and Mai arrive at school. They go straight to the dressing room to get ready. They wait behind the curtain.

Mai "Carly, I don't think I can do this. Look at everyone else. They all look like real pros."

The girls peek out to see the crowd waiting for the show to begin. Their brothers are in the front row.

Carly "Look at us. We look like penguins."

Mai "I don't think I want to do this anymore."

Carly "Let's get outta here! Quick, we can use the back door."

Just then there is an announcement:
*"Ladies, gentlemen, boys, and girls,
our first contestants today are
...Carly and Mai performing as
The Dancing Nuns."* The crowd starts
to cheer.

Carly "Too late to back out now."

The girls look at the stairs that lead to the stage.

Carly "You go first."
Mai "No, you go."
Carly "Just go, you're nearest."

As they walk up the stairs and onto the stage, Carly trips. She drops her tambourine and her foot goes right through the center of it.

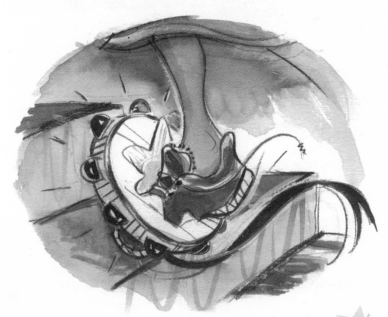

Mai "Oh, no! You all right?"
Carly "Yeah, but..."

The music begins. Mai starts
tapping the tambourine on her hip but
Carly doesn't know what to do—her
tambourine is still stuck on her foot.

CHAPTER 4

What Next?

Carly turns to face Mai and puts her foot up in the air.

Carly (whispering) "Pull it off."

Mai grabs the tambourine and starts
to pull. The tambourine flies up in
the air and both girls fall backward,
landing on their rear ends.

Mai (whispering) "I think I'm gonna
die."

Carly (whispering back) "I know. We'll never be able to show our faces at school again. This is *so* embarrassing."

By now, the crowd is laughing. The girls' brothers are out of their chairs, rolling around on the ground in hysterics. The girls look at each other and stand up.

Carly "What'll we do now? The dance'll never work without the tambourine."

Mai "Let's sing a song."

Carly "What can we sing? We haven't practiced any songs."

Mai "We could try the song 'Maria' from 'The Sound of Music.'"

Carly "Okay."

The girls start to sing.

Mai and Carly *"How do you solve a problem like Maria?"*
Carly (whispering) "What comes next?"
Mai "I'm not sure."
Carly "Listen! The crowd's singing along. They know the words better than us. Let's just sing with them."

Mai "Wow! Everyone's singing with us now!"

As the singing finishes, the crowd cheers—even the girls' brothers. Carly and Mai take a bow, then leave the stage and go back to the dressing room.

CHAPTER 5

Surprise Act

While the other contestants are performing, Carly and Mai sit on the floor in the dressing room grumbling about their performance.

Mai "I think we really messed that up."

Carly "Yeah, thanks to your clumsy act."

Mai "But you were the one that put your foot through the tambourine."

Carly "Maybe, but you made us fall over."

Mai "We're more like The Klutzy Nuns. Or The Stupid Sister Act."

The girls break into fits of laugher as they get back on their feet.

Carly "I hope everybody forgets about the talent show by Monday."

Mai "We should just never go back to school. Maybe we should never even leave our houses again."

Just then a voice comes over the loudspeaker: "*The winner of the talent competition is Carly and Mai, The Singing Nuns.*" The girls look at each other in shock.

Carly "We won! Mr. Prince is calling us for our prize!"

The girls run up on stage.

Mai (whispering) "So, do we make a speech?"

Carly (whispering back) "Yeah, you go first."

Mai "Thanks, everyone. We'll love our dance lessons."

Carly "Yes, thanks a lot. We can't wait to start tap dancing."

Mr. Prince continues over the loudspeaker: *"Thank you, girls, well done. But the dancing lessons you've won are for ballroom dancing, and you'll need to find two male partners to dance with."*

The girls look at each other.

Carly and Mai "Oh, no, not boys! Our sister act's definitely over!"

Mai

GIRLZ ROCK!
Talent Show Lingo

Carly

audience The people who come to watch you perform and hopefully applaud afterward!

costume What you wear to help you portray the character that you are playing.

curtain call When you stay on stage at the end of your show because the audience keeps clapping for a long time. The curtain often opens and closes lots of times, too.

encore When you come back on stage for a repeat performance.

stage fright When you are so afraid of performing on stage that you forget what to do in your performance.

GIRLZROCK!
Talent Show Musts

☆ Practice, practice, practice! You can never practice your act too much.

☆ If you are wearing a costume during your act, make sure it's on properly. You don't want it to fall off while you're on stage!

☆ Even if you're nervous, try to smile.

☆ Make sure your brothers sit at the back of the hall so they can't heckle you or throw things.

☆ Be really careful when you walk onto the stage—tripping is really embarrassing!

☆ Make sure someone videotapes your performance so you can watch it when you get home.

☆ If you put on your own talent show, think about charging a fee for people to see it, and then give the money to a charity.

☆ Ask your parents to sit in the front row so you can see them while on stage. It will help calm your nerves.

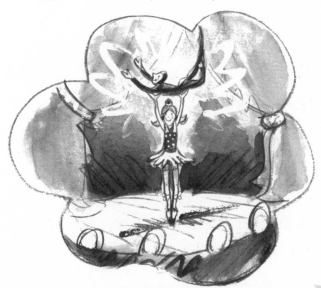

GIRLZ ROCK!
Talent Show
Instant Info

The most popular TV talent show is "American Idol." Around 20 million Americans watch the show every week.

Even if you can't sing or dance, you can still enter a competition. There are kids' contests in art, math, science, writing, and more.

Many talent competitions offer prize money or scholarships to the winners.

When Britney Spears was eight years old, she appeared on the talent competition TV show, *Star Search*. Although she won the first round, she was beaten in the second round!

When someone says "break a leg" before you go on stage, they are wishing you good luck.

Besides Britney Spears, the TV show *Star Search* also helped launch the careers of Ray Romano, LeAnn Rimes, Usher, Justin Timberlake, and Destiny's Child.

GIRLZ ROCK!
Think Tank

1 What is the award for first prize in Carly and Mai's school's talent show?

2 What is the name of Carly and Mai's act in the talent show?

3 Why aren't the girls able to do their dance routine in the talent show?

4 What does it mean when someone says "break a leg" to a performer?

5 What does it mean if you hear "Encore!" being called out by the audience?

6 What do you think would've happened if Carly and Mai had backed out of the talent show?

7 What would you do if you messed up your routine while performing during a talent show?

8 Have you ever gotten stage fright? What did you do to get over it?

Answers

How did you score?

- If you got most of the answers correct, you're ready to be a star performer.

- If you got more than half of the answers correct, being a member of the production crew might be more your style.

- If you got less than half of the answers correct, stay in the audience and practice your loudest clapping.

Hey, Girls!

I hope that you have as much fun reading my story as I have had writing it. I loved reading and writing stories when I was young.

At school, why don't you use "Talent Show" as a play, and you and your friends can be the actors.

Bring in some costumes from home. You can use sheets for the nuns' outfits and some ribbons and tambourines as props. Your school may have a stage where the story could be set.

So...have you decided who is going to be Mai and who is going to be Carly?

Now, with your friends, read and act out this play in front of your classmates. It'll definitely make the whole class laugh.

You can also take the story home and get someone to act out the parts with you.

So, get ready to have more fun reading than a worm has in an apple!

And remember, Girlz Rock!

Sheykettle

Shey talked to Jacqueline, another *Girlz Rock!* author.

Shey "Have you ever been in a talent show?"

Jacqueline "Sure have, and I won first prize!"

Shey "Wow! The other contestants must've been pretty bad."

Jacqueline "There was only one other contestant and she was almost as good as me. But I got the prize."

Shey "Who decided who won?"

Jacqueline "Me—the other contestant was my reflection in the mirror!"

Shey "Ha, you should have won the comedy prize for that!"

GIRLZROCK!
What a Laugh!

Q What's black and white and red all over?

A A nun who forgets her lines on stage.